Pirate Island
Treasure

Pirate Island Treasure

Marilyn Helmer

ILLUSTRATED BY **David Parkins**

ORCA BOOK PUBLISHERS

Library and Archives Canada Cataloguing in Publication

Helmer, Marilyn, author
Pirate island treasure / Marilyn Helmer ;
illustrated by David Parkins.
(Orca echoes)

Issued in print and electronic formats.
ISBN 978-1-4598-0165-3 (pbk.).--ISBN 978-1-4598-0166-0 (pdf).
ISBN 978-1-4598-0519-4 (epub)

I. Parkins, David, illustrator II. Title. III. Series: Orca echoes
PS8565.E4594P57 2013   jc813'.54   C2013-902332-1
                              C2013-902333-X

First published in the United States, 2013
Library of Congress Control Number: 2013937058

Summary: Charlotte, Jacob and their grandpa head off to Pirate Island for an exciting day
of treasure hunting, playing pirates and storytelling.

Orca Book Publishers gratefully acknowledges the support for its publishing programs
provided by the following agencies: the Government of Canada through the Canada Book Fund
and the Canada Council for the Arts, and the Province of British Columbia
through the BC Arts Council and the Book Publishing Tax Credit.

MIX
Paper from
responsible sources
FSC® C004071

ANCIENT FOREST ™
FRIENDLY

*Orca Book Publishers is dedicated to preserving the environment and
has printed this book on Forest Stewardship Council® certified paper.*

Cover artwork and interior illustrations by David Parkins
Author photo by Gary Helmer

ORCA BOOK PUBLISHERS
PO Box 5626, STN. B
Victoria, BC CANADA
v8R 6s4

ORCA BOOK PUBLISHERS
PO Box 468
Custer, WA USA
98240-0468

www.orcabook.com
Printed and bound in Canada.

16 15 14 13 • 4 3 2 1

To Jaxon, Brooklynn, Emily and Ava—
this one's for you!

CHAPTER ONE
Pirate Island

Charlotte ran to the window. "Today's the day!" she shouted. The sun was up, bright and shining. It danced across the waves, scattering shadows along the shore.

She grabbed her binoculars and looked out at the ocean. In the distance was a ribbon of sandy beach. Cliffs rose, dark and mysterious, in the background. Pirate Island. Charlotte felt a shiver of excitement. She could hardly wait to get there. *"Heave ho and away we go, treasure hunting, treasure hunting,"* she sang as she scrambled into her clothes. *"Heave ho and away we go to look for pirate treasure."*

She grabbed her pirate hat from the bedpost and clamped it over her blond curls. She raced up the hall and banged on her brother's door. "Jacob, get up! Today's Pirate Island!"

Grandpa looked up from the stove as Charlotte came into the kitchen. "Good morning, matey," he said. "I thought you were going to sleep all day."

Charlotte shook her head. "Not today, Grandpa. You didn't forget, did you?"

"Was I supposed to remember something?" asked Grandpa.

"We're going treasure hunting today," said Charlotte. "To Pirate Island."

Grandpa looked out the window. "I think it's going to rain."

Charlotte saw the twinkle in Grandpa's eyes. "You're teasing," she said. "The weather's perfect. Sunshine, white puffy clouds and no high waves." She took some dishes from the cupboard and began to set the table.

Jacob came into the kitchen. "I smell blueberry pancakes," he said.

Grandpa piled the pancakes onto a plate. "We can't go treasure hunting on an empty stomach. Dig in, mateys. Then we're off to Pirate Island."

"All right," Jacob cheered.

"Heave ho and away we go, treasure hunting, treasure hunting," Charlotte sang. *"Heave ho and away we go to look for pirate treasure."*

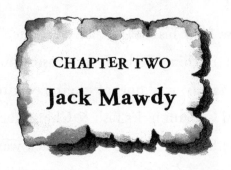

CHAPTER TWO
Jack Mawdy

With breakfast over, everyone scrambled to get ready. Grandpa hurried off to prepare *The Seawind* for departure. Charlotte washed the dishes while Jacob dried them and put them away.

Jacob put the last plate into the cupboard. "Come on, let's go."

"Don't forget your backpack," said Charlotte.

"Got it," said Jacob.

They locked the door and hurried toward the beach.

When they came in sight of the dock, Charlotte said, "Uh-oh. Grandpa's talking to Jack Mawdy."

Jacob grinned. "This could take awhile if Jack starts telling stories."

"I know. I love his stories," said Charlotte, "but today isn't for storytelling. Today is for treasure hunting."

Jack Mawdy was one of their favorite people. He owned Captain Jack's Fish & Chips shop. Captain Jack's was famous for two things. Jack was the best fish-and-chips cook in the county, and he was also the best storyteller. People came from all over to eat Jack's fish and chips and listen to his stories.

Jack saw them and waved them over. "Come see what I found." A hat lettered *Head Chef* sat atop his wiry gray hair. A thick mustache curled around his ruddy cheeks. His blue eyes twinkled beneath bushy eyebrows.

Charlotte loved Jack's stories. She had already decided that one day she would be a famous storyteller too.

Jack held out his hand. "Do you know what this is?"

Charlotte and Jacob examined the object. It looked like a small leather case. Spiny tails trailed from each corner.

"It's an egg case from a skate fish," said Jacob.

"Some people call it a mermaid's purse," Charlotte said. "That's the name I like best."

"Me too." Jack chuckled. "There isn't much of a story in a fish-egg case. But a mermaid's purse, now that's sea treasure, and there's always a story in sea treasure. In fact, I'm thinking of one right now."

Jacob shot Charlotte an *uh-oh* look.

"But I'll save it for later," said Jack. "I hear you're off to do some treasure hunting today."

Grandpa nodded. "We had best get going, but we'll be by for fish and chips later." He winked at Charlotte and Jacob. "Avast, mateys, *The Seawind* is waiting."

As they headed for the dock, Charlotte turned and waved at Jack.

"Don't forget — there are many different kinds of treasure," Jack called to her. "And a story to go with every one."

CHAPTER THREE
Hawk, Shark and Captain Patch Eye

The Seawind cut through the swell, splashing up ocean spray. Gulls circled lazily overhead. Sun tipped the bouncing waves with silver. Charlotte was too excited to notice. "Can't we go faster?" she begged.

"We're almost there," Grandpa called over the engine noise.

Closer to the beach, Grandpa turned off the engine and dropped anchor. He climbed over the side and down a ladder to a rubber dinghy.

"All aboard," he called up to Charlotte and Jacob.

Charlotte climbed down the ladder first. Jacob was right behind her.

When they reached the shore, they pulled the dinghy high onto the sandy beach. They shrugged out of their life jackets and grabbed their backpacks.

"The tide's out," said Jacob.

"It's the best time for treasure hunting," said Charlotte.

Grandpa tied the dinghy to a large rock. "Everybody ready?"

"Let's go!" Charlotte's voice drowned out Jacob's.

"What do you think we'll find?" Jacob didn't wait for an answer. "Maybe caves? Or secret hideouts?"

"Wait." Charlotte stopped. "If we're going to look for pirate treasure, we have to have pirate names."

Jacob spoke quickly, before Charlotte could choose first. "My name is Shark," he growled in a piratey voice.

"I'm Patch Eye," said Charlotte. "Captain Patch Eye, commander of the pirates."

Jacob rolled his eyes. Leave it to Charlotte to take the best job, he thought.

"Grandpa, you need a name too," said Charlotte.

Grandpa thought for a moment. "I'll be Hawk," he said.

Charlotte took the lead. "Shark and Hawk, follow Captain Patch Eye. We're off to find pirate treasure."

Jacob glared at Charlotte's back. Sometimes Charlotte was the bossiest sister in the world.

Beyond the beach, windblown trees grew among the rocks and grasses. The beach was scattered with bits of flotsam and jetsam that had been caught between the stones and sand. The breeze carried a fishy, seaweedy smell.

Jacob picked up a broken toy boat. He tossed an old shoe out of the way.

"Look out for jellyfish," Grandpa warned. He sat down on a large rock and took out his sketchbook. Grandpa liked drawing even more than he liked treasure hunting.

Charlotte picked her way across the rocks and stones. Something caught her eye. She picked it up.

13

"I found a sand dollar," she shouted. Grandpa and Jacob came over to look.

In Charlotte's hand lay a flat shell, round and white as snow. In the middle, five oval lines spread out like flower petals.

"I'll bet I can find one too," said Jacob. "I'll bet I can find a whole bunch of sand dollars."

He hurried ahead of Charlotte, searching the sand. All he saw were plain old clam and crab shells. Wait. A sand dollar! Jacob snatched it up, then quickly tossed it aside. The sand dollar was broken.

He glanced over his shoulder to see where Charlotte was. She saw him and gave a thumbs-up. "I found four more. Two big ones and two little ones."

Grandpa put his sketchbook into his backpack. "Ahoy, mateys. Let's walk on up the beach and see what other treasures we can find."

Charlotte caught up with Jacob and showed him her sand dollars.

Jacob examined them. "Can I have one?"

Charlotte chewed her bottom lip. "Ma-a-a-y-be," she said, dragging out the word.

Jacob kicked the sand. Charlotte's "maybe" usually meant "no." She was being mean. She didn't want to share.

Fine, Jacob told himself. Wait until I have something she wants. Then we'll see who can be mean.

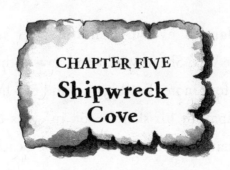

CHAPTER FIVE

Shipwreck Cove

"Ahoy, cove ahead," Charlotte shouted.

"You don't have to shout," said Jacob. "We're right beside you."

He spotted an old fallen tree lying in the sand. It was narrow at one end and split partway down the middle. It reminded Jacob of the hull of an abandoned fishing boat he had seen near the dock.

Jacob ran and jumped onto the narrow end. "Avast, mateys. This is a pirate ship." He caught Charlotte's eye with a fierce look. "And it's under my command."

Charlotte shook her head. "I'm the pirate captain," she said, "so I'm in command."

16

Jacob jumped down. "Rock, Paper, Scissors," he said. It was their favorite way of settling arguments.

"Two out of three," said Charlotte.

Jacob won. "From now on, call me *Captain* Shark," he said with a triumphant grin.

Charlotte gave in. You couldn't argue with Rock, Paper, Scissors.

She stared at the log. Jacob was right. It did look like a pirate ship. A shipwrecked pirate ship. "Grandpa, does this cove have a name?" she asked.

Grandpa shook his head. "Not that I know of."

"Let's call it Shipwreck Cove," said Charlotte. Jack Mawdy's words flew into her head. Treasure…stories…

Ideas whirled through her mind, spinning themselves into a story. "On a dark night long ago, there was a terrible storm," Charlotte began. "Lightning flashed. Thunder roared. Waves rolled in, as high as mountains. Rain pelted down." Charlotte borrowed some of Jack's storytelling words. "The pirates' ship…" She paused, searching for a name.

Jacob jumped in. "*The Treasure Hunter.*" Charlotte wasn't going to have all the storytelling glory.

"Good one, Jacob," said Charlotte. "*The Treasure Hunter* was wrecked in this cove. Captain Shark, Patch Eye and Hawk were stranded on Pirate Island."

"What happened next?" asked Jacob.

"Let's find out," said Charlotte.

CHAPTER SIX
Patch Eye's Spyglass

Jacob picked up a flat stone. He drew back his arm and spun the stone toward the ocean. The stone skipped once, twice, three times before it sank. "Bet you can't beat three skips," he said to Charlotte.

Charlotte never said no to a challenge. She searched until she spotted a black stone, smooth and flat — the best kind for skipping.

As she reached for it, another stone caught her eye. It was small and pale gray. It looked like an ordinary stone, but there was something unusual about it.

Charlotte picked it up. "There's a hole in this stone. I can see right through it."

"Let me have a look," said Jacob.

Charlotte handed him the stone. Jacob held it up to his eye. He had never seen a stone with a hole through it before. Why did Charlotte have to find all the best things?

"Let Grandpa see," said Charlotte.

Jacob passed the stone to Grandpa.

Grandpa examined it. He pointed to the little circles that went all the way through the hole. "It's a fossil," he said. "From an insect or a snail that lived long ago."

"No-o-o," said Charlotte. She reached for the stone and held it up to her eye again. "It's a spyglass. Patch Eye's spyglass."

"Only pirate captains have spyglasses," said Jacob. "I'll bet Patch Eye stole it from Captain Shark."

"Yes," Charlotte said excitedly. "That's exactly what happened. One night, when Captain Shark was asleep, Patch Eye stole the spyglass. She buried it in the sand to keep it safe. But when she came back for it the next day —"

"She couldn't find where she had buried it," Jacob said.

"Years passed," continued Charlotte. "Waves washed the sand away. Then Patch Eye found the spyglass again."

Jacob held out his hand. "But it belongs to Captain Shark."

Charlotte closed her hand. "It belongs to Patch Eye now."

"Rock, Paper, Scissors," said Jacob.

Charlotte shook her head. She wasn't about to lose again.

"Can I borrow it?" Jacob asked.

Charlotte thought for a moment. "Ma-a-a-y-be."

Jacob stomped off. As usual, "maybe" really meant "no." He had to find a way to even things up.

CHAPTER SEVEN

A Deal

Jacob stopped to examine a rock. It was covered with tiny white circles that looked like buttons. Barnacles, Jacob said to himself. But barnacles weren't treasure. He walked on by.

Grandpa sat down on a log to do more sketching. Jacob looked ahead. Farther up the beach, Charlotte was kneeling in the sand. She was looking at something. Jacob caught up with her. "What did you find?"

Charlotte shrugged. "More clam shells." She tossed them aside.

Jacob kneeled beside her. "Ouch!" Something jabbed his knee. He pulled a slim piece of wood from the sand.

Charlotte glanced at it. "It's just an old piece of driftwood."

Jacob stared at the driftwood. "Maybe not." The end he was holding was rounded, like a handle. The other end was thin and smooth. He ran his fingers along the smooth edge. "It feels like a knife blade."

Charlotte reached for it. As she turned it over, the sun caught the smooth edge, turning it a dull silver. "You're right, Jacob. It does look like a knife."

"Not a plain old knife," said Jacob. Charlotte wasn't the only storyteller in the family. "It's a pirate's cutlass. It belonged to Captain Shark. He stuck it in the sand to warn other pirates to stay away."

Charlotte stood up. "But Captain Shark let Patch Eye borrow it," she said. She stuck it into her belt.

"No way." Jacob scrambled to his feet. "You wouldn't let me borrow the spyglass. The cutlass is mine. Give it back." He made a grab for it.

Charlotte stepped back. Stuck in her belt, Jacob's driftwood almost looked like a real cutlass.

She wanted to keep it, at least for a while. "Deal," she said. "I'll give you two of my sand dollars if you let me borrow the cutlass."

Jacob wanted those sand dollars. And he wanted to keep the cutlass. This way he could do both.

He looked Charlotte straight in the eye. "You'll give the cutlass back, right? And I get to keep the sand dollars. Promise? For sure, for certain?"

"Promise. For sure, for certain," Charlotte said solemnly. She got two sand dollars from her backpack and handed them to Jacob. They were the two small ones.

"No way." Jacob shook his head. "I get to choose."

Charlotte took out the other three. Jacob chose two big ones. He put them carefully into his backpack. "Don't forget," he told Charlotte. "I'm only lending you the cutlass. You have to give it back to me."

"I promise. For sure, for certain," said Charlotte.

Jacob was satisfied. He pulled the brim of his ballcap lower on his forehead. Charlotte never broke a for sure, for certain promise. Now he had two sand dollars and a cutlass.

This time Jacob took the lead. *"Heave ho and away we go, treasure hunting, treasure hunting,"* he sang. *"Heave ho and away we go to look for more pirate treasure."*

CHAPTER EIGHT
Something Lost

Charlotte grabbed Jacob's arm. "See those big rocks over there? One of them looks like a face. A fierce face."

Jacob glanced at the rocks. The tallest one was rough and craggy. It did look like a face. Sort of.

"Let's have a closer look," said Charlotte.

Jacob pulled away. "I'm going down by the water."

Charlotte shrugged and headed for the rocks.

Jacob walked along the shore, poking through the pebbles and shells swept in by the tide. One caught his eye. He picked it up. It wasn't a pebble. It was a piece of glass, polished by the waves.

Jacob held it up to the sun. The surface was hazy, pale purple like amethyst. The edges were rounded and smooth.

This was a find! Were there more? Yes. Jacob found three that were as green as sea grass. Then a blue one, a pink, two whites and an amber.

"Ahoy, Jacob!" Grandpa waved at him. "Snack time."

"Coming." Jacob dug a small bag from his backpack. He put the pieces carefully inside. No way was he going to chance losing them. He raced to Grandpa, waving the bag. "Look what I found."

Grandpa looked at the pieces of polished glass. A grin spread across his face. "My brother and I used to collect these," he said. "We called them sea jewels."

Jacob let out a whoop. "Sea jewels! Pirate treasure!" He looked around. "Where is Charlotte?"

"Here she comes," said Grandpa.

Charlotte came around the side of the high, craggy rocks.

"Look what I found, Charlotte. Sea jewels! Real pirate treasure!"

Charlotte barely glanced at them. "They're nice," she said.

Jacob glared at Charlotte. "They're nice? That's all you can say?"

Charlotte shrugged.

What's the matter with her? Jacob wondered. He put the sea glass back into the bag and zipped it into his backpack. He felt a flicker of satisfaction. She's jealous because she didn't find the sea jewels herself, he decided.

Charlotte slumped on a flat rock. Jacob sat beside Grandpa and ignored her.

Grandpa took three crisp apples and bottles of water from his backpack. He offered an apple and water to Charlotte, but she shook her head. "No, thanks, Grandpa."

"Are you feeling all right, matey?" Grandpa asked.

"I'm okay," Charlotte replied. She didn't sound okay though.

Grandpa dug into his backpack again. He pulled out a bag of oatmeal-raisin cookies.

"All right!" said Jacob. Oatmeal-raisin was his favorite kind. He helped himself to three.

Grandpa held the bag out to Charlotte.

Charlotte looked away. "No, thank you, Grandpa. I'm not hungry."

Jacob stared. Charlotte? Saying no to a cookie? Ve-e-e-ry strange.

He put Charlotte out of his mind as he ate the cookies. Right now everything was going his way. He had two perfect sand dollars and the sea-glass jewels. So what if Charlotte wasn't impressed? Best of all, he had his cutlass. Wait. Charlotte had his cutlass. It was time to get it back.

Charlotte sat across from him, staring at her feet.

"I want my cutlass back," said Jacob.

Charlotte didn't answer.

Jacob jumped to his feet. "You promised. For sure, for certain." His freckles stood out like angry dots. "I want my cutlass back, Charlotte. Right now."

Charlotte looked up. "I can't give it back," she said. "I lost it. I've looked everywhere, but I can't find it." Her shoulders sagged. "Jacob, your cutlass is gone."

CHAPTER NINE
The Search

Jacob's face flushed an angry red. "I didn't want to lend you my cutlass in the first place. It was my best find. How could you have lost it?"

Tears welled in Charlotte's eyes. "I'm really, really sorry, Jacob."

Grandpa stood up. "We'll all look for the cutlass. Three pairs of eyes are better than one." He put a hand on Charlotte's shoulder. "Where did you last have it?"

"Over there." She pointed. "By the fierce-faced rock."

They searched around the rocks. They sifted through sand, examining every stick and piece of wood they found. None looked like Captain Shark's cutlass.

Jacob kicked over a flat rock. "We're never going to find it," he said. "My cutlass is gone forever."

Grandpa pulled off his cap and wiped his forehead. "I'm afraid you're right, Jacob."

"Come see this," Charlotte called.

Jacob spun around. Had she found his cutlass?

No, she hadn't. Charlotte was standing on a pile of rocks, tugging at a large wooden object.

"It's just an old lobster trap," Jacob said crossly, but curiosity brought him over for a closer look.

The lobster trap was weathered to a silvery gray sheen. It was in perfect condition except for a broken cross slat. That could easily be fixed. Jacob looked away so Charlotte wouldn't see how much he liked it.

But Charlotte knew. "Captain Shark was cross with Patch Eye for losing his cutlass," she began. "Patch Eye searched and searched, but she couldn't find it. Then she found something else. Something special. And she gave it to Captain Shark."

Jacob shrugged, pretending he didn't care.

"We can clean it up," said Charlotte. "You can put it in your room with the fisherman's net with all your shells on it."

Jacob shrugged again. He clamped his lips to keep from smiling. The lobster trap would be a great addition to his collection.

Grandpa had moved on up the beach.

"Let's catch up with Grandpa," said Charlotte. "We can leave the lobster trap here and get it on the way back."

Jacob didn't answer. He wasn't quite ready to forgive her yet.

Finally, Charlotte gave up and ran ahead. As she ran, something fell out of her pocket, but Charlotte didn't notice.

Jacob hurried over to see what she had dropped. He picked it up. A grin spread right across his face. He put the object into his pocket and closed the zipper. Now he and Charlotte were even.

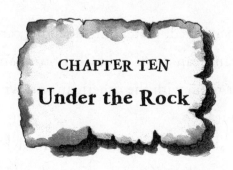

CHAPTER TEN
Under the Rock

Jacob caught up with Charlotte and Grandpa. "The beach is getting narrower," he said.

"The tide's coming in," said Grandpa. "It's time we headed back."

Charlotte groaned. "Do we have to?"

"I'm afraid so," said Grandpa. "We don't want to get caught by high tide."

Reluctantly they turned back. Charlotte walked beside Jacob. "I'm really sorry about the cutlass." Her forehead puckered. "Please don't be mad at me anymore, Jacob."

Jacob thought of what was hidden in his pocket. He smiled to himself. "I'm not mad," he said.

Charlotte whooshed out a great sigh of relief. She took off her pirate hat and fanned her face. "I'm so thirsty I could drink seawater."

"Me too," said Jacob.

"No need for that." Grandpa looked ahead. "We'll stop at the rocks and have a quick drink before we head back to the boat."

They sat on a large flat rock that was balanced on top of two other rocks. "It's like a chair," said Charlotte. "There's room for all of us."

Grandpa opened his backpack. He took out three bottles of water. He handed one to Charlotte and one to Jacob.

Jacob opened his bottle and took a long, thirsty gulp. He was about to set it down when the bottle slipped through his fingers. As he grabbed for it, his foot accidentally kicked it under the rock they were sitting on.

"I'll get it," said Charlotte. She knelt and pulled out the water bottle. "There's something else in here too." She lay on her stomach and reached farther.

Jacob crouched beside her. "What is it?"

Charlotte held it up. "It's just an old bottle," she said, disappointed.

Jacob reached for the bottle. He held it up to the light. It was a soft greeny-blue, the color of the sea.

"That's an old one," said Grandpa. "See the bubbles in the glass?"

Charlotte and Jacob looked closer. Sure enough, there were tiny bubbles all through the glass.

"I think it's broken," said Jacob. "The bottom feels rough."

Grandpa took the bottle. "This one is a real oldie," he said. "It's handblown. That's why it's rough on the bottom." He nodded. "This really is a treasure."

Jacob wasn't convinced. "What use is an old empty bottle?"

Charlotte stared at it. "This isn't any old bottle. This was Captain Shark's bottle. He put a secret message in it. The message said —"

"Stop!" Jacob ordered. "I'm Captain Shark, and I'm the only one who knows what the message said."

CHAPTER ELEVEN
Treasure Chest

"Tell us," said Charlotte. "Come on, Jacob. What did the message say?"

"The message," Jacob began in a rough, piratey voice, "said 'Find the treasure chest.'"

Charlotte threw her arms in the air. "What treasure chest?"

Jacob grinned. "That's for you to figure out."

"Give me a clue," said Charlotte.

Jacob shook his head. "No way. Pirates don't give clues."

"We'll keep a sharp eye out as we walk back to the boat," said Grandpa.

Charlotte set off at a brisk pace, determined to find the treasure chest.

A bit farther on, they came to the lobster trap. As Grandpa picked it up, Jacob whispered something to him. Charlotte didn't notice. Finding the treasure chest was the only thing on her mind.

When they reached the dinghy, Charlotte turned to Jacob. "I give up. Is there really a treasure chest?" She gave him a suspicious look. "Or is this some kind of trick?"

Jacob was pleased with himself. It wasn't often he was able to fool Charlotte. "Grandpa's got the treasure chest," he said.

Charlotte looked as Grandpa set the lobster trap on the sand. "That can't be a treasure chest. There isn't any treasure in it."

Jacob opened the pocket of his backpack. "Put out your hands."

Charlotte cupped her hands. Jacob put the bag of sea glass into them. "Pirates' jewels," he said.

This time Charlotte really looked at them. "They're beautiful," she gasped.

"That's the treasure," said Jacob.

Charlotte sucked in her breath. "Wait. There's more treasure." She dug into her pocket and added the sand dollars to the bag. "Silver dollars. Like pirate coins."

Jacob put his sand dollars in too. "What else do we have?"

"The spyglass," said Charlotte.

She searched one pocket, then the other. Her hands came out empty. She did a frantic search of her backpack. "Oh, no!" She let out a wail of despair. "I've lost Patch Eye's spyglass too!"

CHAPTER TWELVE
Captain Shark's Treasure Map

"First I lost Captain Shark's cutlass," Charlotte groaned. "Now I've lost Patch Eye's spyglass." Her shoulders slumped like an empty sack. "I am the world's worst pirate!"

Jacob hesitated. Should he tell her? Suddenly, getting even didn't seem like fun anymore. He took the holed stone from his pocket.

Charlotte gasped. "What…where did you get it?"

"It fell out of your pocket," said Jacob. "So I picked it up."

Charlotte glared at him. "Why didn't you tell me?"

Jacob frowned. "I wanted to get even because you lost my cutlass."

"But I didn't mean to," said Charlotte. "And I found a treasure chest for you. That's even better than the cutlass, isn't it?"

Jacob shrugged. "I guess so."

Charlotte crouched by the lobster trap. She put the holed stone into the bag with the sand dollars and the sea glass. "A spyglass, sea jewels, silver dollars… wait a minute. The old bottle. Let's put it in too."

"It's empty," said Jacob. "It should have something in it."

Charlotte thought for a moment. "But what?"

"A treasure map," said Jacob.

Charlotte sat back on her heels. "Awesome idea." She looked around. "We need something to draw on."

"Hawk to the rescue," said Grandpa. He took a pencil and his sketchbook from his backpack. "Who's going to draw the treasure map?"

"Me!" Charlotte and Jacob reached for the sketchbook at the same time. Charlotte let her hand drop.

"Captain Shark can draw the map because he's the captain," she said. "Besides, he can draw better than Patch Eye."

Jacob sat in the dinghy. He wrote *Captain Shark, Patch Eye and Hawk's Treasure Map* in crooked letters across the top. Then he drew Pirate Island. He drew pictures in the places they found the sand dollars, the pirate ship, the cutlass, the sea jewels, the lobster trap and the old bottle.

"Perfect," Charlotte declared when he was finished.

Jacob tore the map out of the sketchbook. He looked at it this way and that. "It doesn't look like a real treasure map." Carefully, he tore around the sides of the map. Now the edges were rough and uneven. "That's much better."

Charlotte looked over his shoulder. "It's too clean," she said. "A treasure map that's been in an old bottle would be grungy." She stood up. "Help me find some seaweed."

"What for?" asked Jacob.

"You'll see," said Charlotte.

They found a clump of dry black seaweed. Charlotte squished it and smeared it all over the map.

Now the map looked grungy and old. It looked like a real treasure map.

"That is one fine treasure map," said Grandpa.

"It's the best-ever treasure map," said Charlotte.

Jacob rolled up the map and put it into the bottle. They were right. It was the best treasure map ever.

CHAPTER THIRTEEN
A Pirate Tale

Charlotte took off her pirate hat and waved. "Goodbye, Pirate Island," she shouted over the noise of *The Seawind*'s engine. "This has been an awesome day."

"It sure has." Jacob leaned against the treasure chest sitting between them.

"I can't wait to show Jack Mawdy what we found," said Charlotte.

"We can tell him about Hawk, Patch Eye and Captain Shark's adventures," Jacob added.

"This time you two will be the storytellers," Grandpa called to them.

Charlotte wiggled in her seat. "We can tell Jack Mawdy our pirate story, Jacob. Let's practice."

She began in a rough, raspy voice. "On a dark, stormy night long ago, three pirates set sail in their ship, *The Treasure Hunter*. The pirates' names were Hawk, Patch Eye and Captain Shark. They were looking for a place to hide their treasure."

"The waves were so high, they couldn't steer the ship," Jacob continued. "Captain Shark looked through his spyglass." He rummaged in the treasure chest for the holed stone and held it up to his eye. "Land ahoy!" he shouted gruffly. "Head for Pirate Island!"

"Then *The Treasure Hunter* got wrecked in Shipwreck Cove." Charlotte took the sand dollars and sea jewels from the treasure chest. "Captain Shark, Patch Eye and Hawk buried their treasure in the sand."

"Captain Shark drew a treasure map," said Jacob. "He put it in an old bottle." He took the bottle from the treasure chest. "Then Captain Shark hid the bottle under a flat rock so no one would find it.

And he stuck his cutlass in the sand to warn other pirates to stay away."

"But Patch Eye stole the cutlass," said Charlotte. "And she lost it. So there was nothing to guard the treasure."

"Then we found it." Jacob put the spyglass and the old bottle back into the treasure chest.

Charlotte put the sea jewels and the sand dollars in too. "Now we have a treasure chest full of treasure."

"As well as a great tale to tell," said Grandpa. "You can tell Jack Mawdy all about it over dinner tonight."

"Fish and chips!" Jacob cheered.

"Chowder and scones," Charlotte shouted. "Can we go faster, Grandpa? I can't wait to get there."

Grandpa laughed and turned the engine to full throttle.

"Heave ho and away we go, treasure hunting, treasure hunting," Charlotte sang in her loudest voice. Jacob and Grandpa quickly joined in. *"Heave ho and back we go with tales of pirate treasure."*

Marilyn Helmer is the author of many books for children, including picturebooks, early readers, novels, riddle books and retold tales. She discovered a knack for storytelling at a very young age, making up wild and creative excuses for the occasional bout of mischief. *Pirate Island Treasure* is her sixth book with Orca and her fifth in the Orca Echoes series. Marilyn and her husband live near Belwood, Ontario. For more information, visit www.marilynhelmer.com.